ADIÓS,
ANNA

YEARLING BOOKS are designed especially to entertain and enlighten young people. Patricia Reilly Giff, consultant to this series, received her bachelor's degree from Marymount College and a master's degree in history from St. John's University. She holds a Professional Diploma in Reading and a Doctorate of Humane Letters from Hofstra University. She was a teacher and reading consultant for many years, and is the author of numerous books for young readers.

Adiós, Anna

PATRICIA REILLY GIFF

Illustrated by DyAnne DiSalvo-Ryan

A YEARLING BOOK

Special thanks to Jean Rincón,
Spanish specialist at
Hunter Elementary School
in New York City.

Published by
Bantam Doubleday Dell Books for Young Readers
a division of
Bantam Doubleday Dell Publishing Group, Inc.
1540 Broadway
New York, New York 10036

ISBN: 0-440-41070-3

Printed in the United States of America

August 1995

10 9 8 7 6 5

TO THE WORLD'S GREATEST KIDS:

Jimmy
Chrissie
Billy
and
Caitie

Where to Find the Spanish Lessons in This Book

ADIÓS, ANNA

DOS Y DOS SON CUATRO

Dos y dos son cuatro,
Two and two are four,

cuatro y dos son seis,
Four and two are six,

seis y dos son ocho,
Six and two are eight,

y ocho, dieciseis.
And eight are sixteen.

1

Sarah Cole tiptoed down the back steps.

She stepped over Gus, her huge yellow dog.

She sneaked across the driveway.

If she made one sound, she'd be stuck with her little sister Erica . . . and with skinny Thomas Attonichi.

Sarah looked back.

Erica was swinging on a tree branch.

Skinny Thomas was swinging, too.

They'd break the branch any minute.

They'd break their necks.

"Hey," Sarah yelled.

Erica stopped swinging. "We're coming with you."

"No good," said Sarah.

The screen door banged open.

"Errrricaaaa," Aunt Minna yelled.

Sarah began to run.

Anna Ortiz was waiting at the corner. Anna, who was leaving for camp tomorrow.

Anna, her best friend in the whole world.

"Dos y dos son cuatro," Anna was singing.

She was balancing her library book on her head.

"Hola, Sarah," she shouted.

"Hurry," Sarah shouted back. "I just got away from Erica and Thomas."

They took the library shortcut . . . through the alley, behind Sarah's mother's bakery.

They made believe they were Spanish dancers.

"*Dos y dos . . . ,*" they sang.

Anna's mother had taught it to them.

"Wait a minute." Sarah stopped.

Someone else was taking the shortcut.

It was Benjamin Bean from their class, grinning at them, half a banana in his mouth.

Benjamin, the worst pest in the world.

Worse than Erica and skinny Thomas put together.

Benjamin twirled on his toes. "*Dos y dos,*" he sang with his mouth full.

"*Dos y dos,*" someone else sang.

It was Erica . . . clicking along in Aunt Minna's high heels.

Skinny Thomas was right behind her.

Thomas wasn't singing, though.

Thomas never even talked.

"Do you have to follow us all over the place?" Sarah asked.

Sarah and Anna marched up the steps. Anna opened the library door.

"*Dos y dos,*" Benjamin sang.

He looked as if he hadn't washed since school closed.

"*Cara de plátano,*" Anna said.

"What?" Sarah asked.

Benjamin leaned forward.

Anna laughed. "Banana face," she whispered.

They walked past the librarian's desk.

"I wish I knew Spanish," said Sarah.

Anna nodded. "We could talk and talk. Banana mouth wouldn't know one word."

"Like a secret language," Sarah said.

"Yes." Anna's eyes opened wide. "There's a book. *El español en diez días.*" Where did I see? . . ."

"But what does that mean?" Erica asked.

Anna stood up. " 'Spanish in ten days.' "

She raced for the shelves.

Sarah raced after her.

So did Benjamin.

Erica clicked along behind with Thomas.

Sarah and Benjamin grabbed the book at the same time.

"I got it first," he said.

"You did not." Sarah gave it a tug.

She tried not to touch his fingers.

They had banana all over them.

The librarian, Mrs. Muñoz, came toward them.

She took the book. "*¿El español en diez días?*" She smiled. "*Bueno.*"

"That means all right," Anna said.

Mrs. Muñoz handed the book to Sarah.

"All right. *Diez días* for you," she said. "And then *diez días* for him."

"*Bueno*," said Erica.

Sarah gritted her teeth. Not so *bueno*.

She felt like punching Benjamin right in his . . . She thought for a moment . . . *cara de plátano.*

"Make sure," the librarian said to Sarah. "Have this book back in ten days."

Sarah nodded.

She'd have to study hard. Learn the whole thing before Anna came home from camp.

Before Benjamin got his hands on the book.

Benjamin was the smartest kid in their class.

He'd probably know the whole thing in just nine days.

Los colores (los co-LOR-ehs)	**The Colors**
rojo (ROH-hoh)	red
azul (ah-SOOL)	blue
verde (VER-deh)	green
amarillo (ah-ma-REE-yoh)	yellow
anaranjado (ah-na-ran-HA-doh)	orange
violeta (vee-oh-LEH-tah)	purple
pardo (PAR-doh)	brown
blanco (BLAHN-coh)	white
negro (NEH-groh)	black

2

Sarah knew she was sleeping. Dreaming.

Spanish words were floating in her head.

The words she and Anna had worked on yesterday.

Azul . . . rojo . . . verde.   Blue . . . red . . . green.

She tried to open her eyes.

Something was happening.

Maybe it was a hurricane.

She could feel her bed shaking, and rain pouring down on her head.

"I'm drowning," she yelled.

"I'll save you," shouted Erica.

Sarah opened her eyes.

Erica was standing over her. One foot was on Sarah's pillow. Her other foot was on the windowsill.

She was holding the spaghetti pot in her arms.

Water was sloshing out all over the place.

Sarah tried to sit up straight, but Gus was sleeping on her feet. He was wearing Erica's yellow hat with the daisy.

"What are you doing, Erica?" she asked. "The whole bed is wet. I'm wet . . ."

"I'm having a typhoon," Erica said. "Thomas Attonichi had one yesterday."

Erica tilted the pot. "We need some *agua*."

She began to pour water through the screen.

Sarah could hear it splash against the side of the house.

It landed on the ground with a splat.

Erica had followed them around yesterday.

She had said the Spanish words over and over . . . until Sarah wanted to scream.

"Hey," Erica said. "There goes Anna's car."

Sarah jumped out of bed. She knelt at the window with Erica.

Anna stuck her head out of the open car window. "*Adiós,* Sarah!" she called. "I'll miss you."

"*Adiós,* Anna," she called back.

The blue car turned the corner.

The Ortizes were gone. Mr. and Mrs. Ortiz off on a trip. Anna to camp.

And Sarah was stuck.

Stuck with Erica, who had just drowned the seeds she and Anna had planted yesterday.

Stuck with Thomas Attonichi, the kindergarten baby.

Worst of all, she was stuck with Benjamin, *cara de plátano*.

Benjamin, the smartest kid in the class, and the dirtiest.

Benjamin, who was trying to learn Spanish, just because he was nosy.

She threw on her shorts and went down to breakfast.

It was her favorite. Chocolate milk and almost burned toast with jelly.

Aunt Minna was in the kitchen.

She was as skinny as a Q-tip, with a ball of white hair on her head.

Aunt Minna stood in front of a wedding cake, squeezing a bag of icing.

Great swirls of pink poured out over the cake.

Pink loops, and bows, and . . .

Sarah leaned closer. "Is that . . ."

Aunt Minna nodded. "A pickup truck. Something new. Something different."

Sarah smiled. She could see the truck, and a little bride and groom.

It wasn't a real cake. It was a cardboard cake for their bakery window.

Sarah took a bite of her toast.

She thought of Anna.

Anna would be swimming today.

Or going on a hike.

Or having a scavenger hunt—that game where you look for stuff and the first one to find everything gets a prize.

"Sarah?" Aunt Minna said. "Take Erica with you when you go out to play. I'll love you forever."

Erica was in the doorway, putting on her shirt.

It was inside out and backward.

"I'm just going to do Spanish words," Sarah said. She couldn't believe it. In ten days she'd know Spanish. She felt a little worm of worry. Suppose she couldn't do it?

She dropped her crusts down to Gus.

"*Bueno*," said Erica. "I'll do Spanish words, too."

Something else was bothering Sarah.

Something she should remember.

Erica slapped on her hat with the daisy.

It was so big it covered her eyes.

Outside it was hot. It was muddy under the window, with little puddles of water.

Agua.

Then she remembered.

The book . . . *El español en diez días.*

It was locked in Anna's house.

There for the rest of the summer.

EL ESPAÑOL EN DIEZ DÍAS

Los números (los NOOM-eh-rohs)	**The Numbers**
uno (OOH-noh)	one
dos (DOHS)	two
tres (TREHS)	three
cuatro (CWAH-troh)	four
cinco (SING-coh)	five
seis (SEHS)	six
siete (see-EH-teh)	seven
ocho (OH-choh)	eight
nueve (noo-EH-veh)	nine
diez (dee-EHS)	ten

3

"How about we march over to Thomas Attonichi's," said Erica.

Sarah shook her head. "I want to go to Anna's. Maybe . . ."

"Maybe what?"

"Maybe . . . I don't know," Sarah said.

They went across the yard and into the woods.

It really wasn't woods.

It was a leftover space between the houses.

There were a bunch of skinny trees.

Weeds that smelled. A pile of sticker bushes.

"Walk on two toes," Erica told her. "A zillion snails are hanging around in here. Thomas Attonichi said so."

"Thomas Attonichi." Sarah made a snorting sound.

"That's right," Erica said. "You don't want to crack the poor snails' backs."

Thomas might not even know how to talk, Sarah thought.

She walked on her toes anyway.

Gently.

There were blue flowers under the trees.

"*Rojo,*" Sarah said.

Erica shook her head. "That's red. You mean *azul.* Blue."

"Listen, Erica," said Sarah. "If you say one more word . . ."

Erica pressed her lips together hard.

Anna's house was on the other side.

Sarah could see her kitchen door and the back steps.

She peeked in the living room window.

A picture of a mountain hung over the table.

It was just like the ones Sarah drew in school: pointy with snow on top.

Anna's mother had told her she had been born near the mountain . . . far away in Colombia.

Sarah stood on tiptoes.

Erica opened her mouth. "What are you doing, anyway?"

"My book is on the chair," she said.

"El español en diez días," said Erica.

Sarah wiggled the doorknob. Locked.

"Try to open the other window," Erica said. *"La ventana."*

"Don't be smart," Sarah said. "Besides, it's too high."

Sarah bit at her fingernail.

She could taste a little jelly.

She couldn't go into Anna's house anyway.

That would be terrible.

Benjamin and Thomas were in the woods now. She could hear them.

"Let's go, men," Benjamin was shouting at the top of his lungs. *"Vámonos."*

What was that now? Sarah wondered. Something in Spanish? It sounded like VAH-moh-nohs.

He said, 'Let's go,' in Spanish," Erica said.

That Benjamin had some nerve.

She could see Aunt Minna through the trees. She was in the backyard, looking for them.

Then Sarah remembered.

Anna's key.

It was under a rock.

She could open the door fast . . . race inside, and get the book.

She'd be outside, quick as a wink.

She'd spend every single minute working on her Spanish.

Muy bien.

Benjamin was sounding closer now.

Sarah tiptoed to the rock.

She dug for the key, and held it up.

"*La llave,*" she said.

Erica shook her head. "Say YAH-veh."

"Shh." Sarah was in the kitchen in two seconds.

Erica was holding her hat up over one eye to watch.

"This way, men," Benjamin was shouting.

"Sarah . . . Erica . . . ," Aunt Minna was calling.

From the window, Sarah could see Benjamin coming.

She grabbed the book.

She tucked it under her shirt.

She raced out the door.

Benjamin and Thomas were standing there, pointing.

"Thief," said Benjamin. "Maybe we should get the police."

Erica pulled her hat down over her eyes.

Sarah closed the door behind her.

EL ESPAÑOL EN DIEZ DÍAS

La casa
(la CAH-sah)

The House

---

la ventana
(la ven-TAHN-nah)

the window

la puerta
(la PWEHR-tah)

the door

la llave
(la YAH-veh)

the key

la cocina
(la coh-SEE-nah)

the kitchen

la sala
(la SAH-lah)

the living room

el dormitorio
(el dor-mee-TOH-ree-oh)

the bedroom

el baño
(el BAH-nyoh)

the bathroom

4

"Will they put you in jail?" Erica looked as if she were going to cry.

Sarah felt like crying, too. Her mouth was dry. She couldn't talk.

"After them, men," yelled Benjamin.

He galloped across Anna's lawn.

Thomas galloped after him.

"*Vámonos*," yelled Erica.

Sarah grabbed Erica's hand and started to run.

They sped into the woods.

They ducked behind a skinny tree.

Sarah could feel her heart pound.

What would Anna's mother do when she found out?

What would Anna say?

But there was no time to think.

"A robber from outer space," Benjamin shouted. "One who can't speak Spanish."

Sarah opened her mouth. *"Cara de plátano,"* she said under her breath.

"Ssh," whispered Erica.

Sarah couldn't be quiet, though.

A horrible thing was crawling over her sandals.

It was heading for her ankle.

It had a thousand hairy legs.

Sarah screamed so loud she scared everyone.

Aunt Minna jumped over a sticker bush.

She raced toward them.

Benjamin and Thomas dashed away.

They disappeared behind Anna's house.

"What's going on?" Aunt Minna said. "You scared me to death."

Sarah pointed, but the thing was gone.

Her Spanish book was there, though. Dirty with a wrinkled page.

Sarah closed her eyes. If only she were in camp with Anna.

If only her mother hadn't said to wait until next year.

"Don't scream like that," Aunt Minna said.

"I never scream." Erica shook her head. Her earrings danced. "I'm not afraid of a little crawler. Thomas says they're good."

"I'm sick of Thomas," Sarah said.

She looked back.

She could see Benjamin peeking out from the side of Anna's house.

His hair stood up in spikes.

He was crossing his brown, toad eyes.

Suppose he told the police she was a robber?

She swallowed. Benjamin's father was a policeman.

How could she have forgotten that?

Aunt Minna began again. "Get changed. We'll hop in the truck and head over to your mother's bakery."

Sarah sighed. She wouldn't be able to look at her mother.

She'd know something had happened.

Aunt Minna nodded. "We'll drop off the wedding cake. Plunk it down in the bakery window. Everyone will want to get married."

Benjamin inched out from behind Anna's house.

"Let's go," Sarah said.

They followed Aunt Minna to her pickup truck.

Gus was there ahead of them. He was slobbering all over the place.

Sarah helped Erica into the front seat.

"Yuck," said Erica. "The whole seat is wet."

Sarah slid in after her. She tried to sit on a dry spot.

She watched Erica pull off a bracelet.

Erica rolled it up over Gus's leg.

Sarah sat back.

She hadn't put Anna's key back.

Where was it? *La llave* . . .

EL ESPAÑOL EN DIEZ DÍAS

La cara (la CAH-rah)	**The Face**
la cabeza (la cah-BEH-sah)	the head
los ojos (los OH-hohs)	the eyes
la nariz (la nah-REES)	the nose
la boca (la BOH-kah)	the mouth
los dientes (los deeEN-tehs)	the teeth
las orejas (las oh-REH-hahs)	the ears
el pelo (el PEH-loh)	the hair

5

Five days were up. Five to go. *Cinco días.*

Sarah knew the colors in Spanish. Some of them.

She knew the numbers. Maybe.

Erica kept laughing at her.

"Wrong," she'd say every two minutes.

Right now Sarah opened the library door.

She was holding *El español en diez días* under her arm.

It was cleaned. It was ironed.

Only a teeny spot of something was left on page six.

Aunt Minna had fixed it for her.

She needed a place to sit by herself.

Someplace cool.

Someplace quiet.

Sarah was worried. She couldn't stop thinking about Anna's key. And the police.

Inside the library, she tiptoed toward the back.

A bunch of computers were blinking.

Benjamin was sitting at one.

Sarah made believe she didn't see him.

Benjamin was pretending to talk on a phone. "Police? Yeah. She sneaks around in other people's houses. Might be a murderer."

Sarah could hear him laughing . . . cackling.

She made a wide circle around him and sat at an empty table.

She looked across at him.

Benjamin was the best reader in the class.

The best speller.

The best everything.

She tried to remember if he was a tattle-tale.

Benjamin stood up.

He turned off the computer.

The picture faded away.

He wandered over toward her.

"Aroo, aroo, arooooooo," he whispered.

It sounded like a police siren.

The librarian, Mrs. Muñoz, came over, too. *"Hola, ¿cómo estás?"*

Sarah felt her face get hot.

"What?" she asked.

"Muy bien," said Benjamin.

Sarah swallowed. "How do you know all that?"

He pointed to Mrs. Muñoz. "She taught me."

Mrs. Muñoz laughed. "I'm giving him a little head start."

Sarah stood up. She nodded at Mrs. Muñoz.

Mrs. Muñoz smiled.

Sarah walked down the aisle and out of the library.

She felt as if everyone was looking at her.

One thing she knew.

She didn't know how to speak Spanish.

She was terrible at it.

But maybe it didn't even matter.

Soon, Anna wouldn't be her best friend.

And maybe she'd even be in jail!

EL ESPAÑOL EN DIEZ DÍAS

La familia y los amigos	Family and Friends
la familia (la fah-MEE-lee-yah)	the family
los amigos (los ah-MEE-gohs)	the friends
el padre (el PAH-dreh)	the father
la madre (la MAH-dreh)	the mother
el hermano (el er-MAHN-oh)	the brother
la hermana (la er-MAHN-ah)	the sister
el perro (el PEH-rroh)	the dog
el gato (el GAH-toh)	the cat
el pez (el PEHS)	the fish
la mascota (la mas-COH-tah)	the pet

6

It was almost dark.

Sarah sat on her back step with Gus.

She had had a lump in her throat all day.

Her father's flashlight was in her hand. The one he had given her for worm searching.

The light was as big as a flea.

She tried to see the words and pictures in her Spanish book.

She turned the page. *"Casa.* Cah-sah. That's house. And *puerta.* Pwehr-tah. Door."

39

Sarah shivered. She thought about Benjamin. He knew she had opened Anna's door.

And another thing. She had to find *la llave*. It must be in the woods.

Inside the kitchen she could hear soft clicking sounds.

Her mother was typing the bakery list on the computer.

"One hundred pounds of flour," Sarah could hear her say. "Twenty pounds of raisins."

Sarah stretched up.

She could see the green light from the screen and paper sliding out.

Erica was singing with her father.

Sarah wished she could tell her mother . . . or her father . . . about Anna.

Tell them before Benjamin told his father, the policeman.

What would they say?

Next to her, Gus yawned.

Sarah leaned over. She felt his soft ears and his wrinkled neck.

Erica had painted his toenails pink.

"*El pez,*" she told him. "That's you."

Inside, Erica started to laugh. "*Pez* means fish."

"I meant *gato.*"

"Cat," said Erica.

Sarah took a quick look at the book. "*Perro,* I mean."

She sighed.

She should look for *la llave* now.

Before it was really dark. Scary dark.

She gave Gus one last pat. She tiptoed across the yard.

Her father called out the door. "Five minutes, honey."

"All right."

41

"Where are you going, honey?" Erica yelled.

"Nowhere."

"I'll come. I just won't eat my corn."

"Four bites," her mother said.

In the woods, Sarah could see fireflies.

She could hear crickets, and strange noises.

How could she find *la llave* in the dark?

But tomorrow they were going to the pond with Aunt Minna. She wouldn't have time to look.

Sarah picked up a stick and poked it around.

She hoped she wasn't poking some poor snail.

She felt something on her arm.

One of those horrible crawly . . .

No, worse. It was a hand.

She began to scream.

Someone clapped a hand over her mouth.

It smelled like peanut butter.

Benjamin.

"Why are you always screaming?" he asked.

"I'm not," she said.

She shined the flashlight on his face.

Filthy.

"What are you doing out here?" she asked.

"What do you think? My father's a cop. I'm trying to catch robbers."

Someone crashed through the bushes.

Sarah remembered not to scream.

It was Thomas, wearing a Walkman.

In the almost dark he looked like a skinny bug.

And Erica. "Everyone catching fireflies?" she asked.

"Capturing something," Benjamin said.

"*Bueno,*" said Erica. "You can come to the pond tomorrow. I asked Aunt Minna."

Sarah shook her head. But it was too late.

"Good idea." Benjamin nodded. "I can keep my eye on a criminal."

EL ESPAÑOL EN DIEZ DÍAS

La ropa (la ROH-pah)	**Clothing**
la camiseta (la cah-mee-SEH-tah)	the T-shirt
el pantalón (el pahn-tah-LOHN)	the pants
el pantalón corto (el pahn-tah-LOHN COR-toh)	the shorts
los zapatos (los sah-PAH-tohs)	the shoes
los calcetines (los cal-seh-TEEN-ehs)	the socks

7

It was hot and sticky.

Sarah ran upstairs four times.

First for Aunt Minna's sunglasses.

Then for the towels, the bug spray, and her Spanish book.

The whole time Erica was crying.

Screaming.

And Aunt Minna was talking. "You can't wear three necklaces . . ."

"But Thomas loves them," Erica said.

"You're going to lose them," Aunt Minna said.

Sarah dumped the towels in the truck.

Benjamin and Thomas were in the back already . . . just sitting, waiting.

Thomas was wearing his father's fishing hat over his Walkman earphones.

Benjamin was wearing a new shirt. It said: CRIME BUSTERS.

Everyone waited while Erica ran to the woods for a pail she had left.

Then they were on their way.

Aunt Minna drove slowly . . . so slowly Erica thought they'd never get there.

At last they pulled into the parking lot.

The pond was small. Reeds poked out of the top.

A tall slide was in the water.

Too tall for Sarah.

"I bet Anna has a pool at camp," she said.

"Who wants to go to camp, anyway?" Benjamin pulled out his Super Soaker.

"All criminals get a shot of water in the head," he said, but he was laughing.

Sarah moved away from him. She stuck her toes in the edge of the pond.

On the bottom she saw green strings and mud.

Last year she and Anna had gone to the pond every day.

They had screamed when their feet touched the strings.

They never climbed the slide.

It was sad to lose a best friend for a whole summer, Sarah thought.

Worse, if your best friend found out you were a robber.

Benjamin dashed by, splashing water.

He pounded up the slide.

He slid down like a rocket.

When he came up, his face was clean.

Sarah blinked.

He looked nice with a clean face.

"Come on," he said.

She shook her head.

"You're afraid," he said.

"I am not."

"You're always screaming."

Sarah sloshed through the green strings away from him.

"How come you're not afraid to rob houses?" he said.

She was at the slide.

She could hear Erica. "Sarah didn't rob Anna's house. Not exactly. She needed the book. *El español en diez días.*"

Benjamin was right, Sarah thought. She was always afraid.

She put her foot on the rung of the ladder up to the slide. And then the other foot.

She could feel her heart pound.

Then she was at the top.

It was high. Very high.

Down below, she could see Erica. And Thomas.

And Benjamin, calling to her. "Just keep saying you're not afraid."

She slid down . . . faster and faster.

She saw the water coming closer.

She felt the splash.

Aunt Minna was calling, "Good girl, Sarah."

Thomas was smiling.

She took a quick peek at Benjamin.

He was smiling, too.

And Erica was screaming. "Where's my beautiful necklace?"

EL ESPAÑOL EN DIEZ DÍAS

Los días de la semana *(los DEE-as de la se-MAH-nah)*	The Days of the Week
el lunes *(el LOO-nehs)*	Monday
el martes *(el MAR-tehs)*	Tuesday
el miércoles *(el meeEHR-coh-lehs)*	Wednesday
el jueves *(el huEH-vehs)*	Thursday
el viernes *(el veeEHR-nehs)*	Friday
el sábado *(el SAH-bah-doh)*	Saturday
el domingo *(el do-MING-goh)*	Sunday

8

It was Thursday, after lunch.

Erica and Gus were taking a nap.

Sarah walked to the bakery by herself.

She was carrying a sign Aunt Minna had made. It was for the window.

OUR WEDDING CAKES CAN'T BE BEAT.

Sarah talked to herself the whole way.

She hoped no one was watching.

She remembered what Benjamin had said.

"Don't be afraid. Don't be afraid. Don't be . . ."

Benjamin was turning out to be a lot better than she thought.

She looked in the bakery window.

The pickup truck wedding cake was in the middle.

On each side were plates of cookies, and cupcakes with red cherries on top.

Red, Sarah thought. *Rojo.* Roh-ho. And cookies. *Galletas.* Gah-YEH-tahs. At least she thought they were *galletas.*

She opened the bakery door. Inside she could smell bread and cinnamon.

Usually her mouth watered.

But right now it was hard to think about food.

She went toward the back.

Her mother was in there with Manny, the baker.

Sarah wanted to say *hola* to him.

She didn't, though. She'd probably even say *hello* wrong.

Manny smiled at her. He went out to the back steps to have his lunch.

Sarah's mother swooped down to give her a hug.

Flour was on her nose, her arms, her hands.

She smelled like vanilla.

She looked at the sign Sarah had in one hand.

"Great," she said. "We'll hang it over the pickup truck wedding cake."

"Yes." said Sarah.

Don't be afraid. Don't be afraid. Don't . . .

"Let's have milk and rye bread ends," her mother said. "And . . ."

Sarah nodded.

". . . you can tell me what's the matter."

"How did you know . . . ," Sarah began.

Her mother patted her shoulder.

The bell jingled.

A woman came in and bought three cupcakes.

Sarah fixed the tray again.

You couldn't tell that any of the cupcakes had been sold.

Then it was quiet again.

Her mother cut the end of a rye bread loaf.

She poured two glasses of milk.

Sarah sat at one end of the floury table.

Don't be afraid. Don't . . .

Her mother turned her head to one side. "What are you trying to say?"

Sarah looked down at the little seeds in the rye bread.

She counted them.

Four . . . five . . . six.   *Cuatro . . . cinco . . . seis.*

Her mother began again. "What did you say?"

Sarah looked to the front.

No one there.

No one to hear she was a robber.

"I meant to tell you," Sarah said, "I went down the slide."

Her mother took a bite of bread. "Wonderful. Brave. I'm proud."

"I'm trying not to be afraid," Sarah said.

Then she told the whole story in a rush. *El español en diez días.* Anna's house. *La llave.*

Sarah looked down at the rye bread again. It was hard to catch her breath.

She waited to hear what her mother would say.

EL ESPAÑOL EN DIEZ DIAS

La carta (la CAR-tah)	**The Letter**
el lápiz (el LAH-pees)	the pencil
la pluma (la PLOO-mah)	the pen
el papel (el pah-PEL)	the paper
el sello (el SEH-yoh)	the stamp
el sobre (el SOH-breh)	the envelope
el libro (el LEE-broh)	the book

9

Sarah was sitting on her bed.

She could hear Erica outside. Erica was talking to Thomas.

Sarah had just written a letter to Anna.

The letter was her mother's idea.

Her mother had wonderful ideas.

Mrs. Cole said she'd send one letter to Mr. and Mrs. Ortiz.

And Sarah could send another to Anna.

Sarah went over to the window.

She had written to Anna in her best handwriting.

Hola, Anna,

    I miss you. I went in your casa
for my libro. I won't go in again.
    Adiós.

                 Sarah

Outside Sarah could see Benjamin coming.

She took one last look.

She could see little bits of green underneath the window.

Sunflowers.

They were coming up after all.

She went down the stairs and out the back.

She had a wonderful idea, too.

Benjamin was sitting on the step now.

So was Thomas.

Erica was combing Gus's small tail.

"We're going to have a scavenger hunt," Sarah said.

"What's that?" Benjamin asked.

"It's when you look for stuff," she said. "With a prize for the person who finds everything."

Thomas looked up.

"Thomas wants to know what the prize is," said Erica.

Sarah thought fast.

"A doughnut."

"I'm going home," said Benjamin.

"Please don't go home," she said. "We have to find *la llave*."

"Some robber," said Benjamin. "You even lost the key?"

Sarah nodded.

Benjamin thought for a minute. "All right. We'll find the key. Then you'll never rob a house again."

"Never," said Sarah.

"We'll be able to close the case," Benjamin said.

"Yes," said Sarah.

"And . . ." Benjamin leaned forward, grinning. "We'll share *El español en diez días*. Learn the words together."

Now it was Sarah's time to think. "Why not?" she said. "I have the book. You say the words better than me. We'll do it together."

They started at the first tree.

Even Gus came with them.

Thomas crawled through the bushes.

He was the first one to find something. A small tan snail.

Benjamin was next. "Hey." He held up Erica's necklace.

"That's where it was," said Erica. "I dropped it when I took my pail."

Gus found something, too.

An old bone from last summer.

But no key.

Not under the trees, the sticker bushes, or the weeds.

Thomas found it at the last minute.

It was on the edge of Anna's lawn.

"*La llave.*" Sarah smiled.

"This is just as good as camp," she said. "We went to the pond this week, we had a scavenger hunt, and snacks . . ."

Benjamin nodded. "And a crime."

They could hear Aunt Minna calling. "Raisin bread and milk."

"*Pan.* And *leche*," said Sarah. "Even I know that."

Erica nodded.

"Come on, then," Sarah said. "Let's go, *amigos.*"

POSTCARD FROM ANNA:

2 de agosto

Hola, Sarah,
 You are still my best amiga!
 I can't wait to come home.
 Adiós,

 Anna

Sarah Cole
185-02 143 Ave.
Springfield, New York

EL ESPAÑOL EN DIEZ DÍAS

Los meses del año *(lohs MEH-sehs dehl AH-nyoh)*	**The Months of the Year**
enero *(eh-NEH-roh)*	January
febrero *(feh-BREH-roh)*	February
marzo *(MAHR-soh)*	March
abril *(ah-BREEL)*	April
mayo *(MAH-yoh)*	May
junio *(HOO-neeoh)*	June
julio *(HOO-leeoh)*	July
agosto *(ah-GOH-stoh)*	August
septiembre *(sehp-TYEHM-breh)*	September
octubre *(ohk-TOO-breh)*	October
noviembre *(noh-VYEHM-breh)*	November
diciembre *(dee-SYEHM-breh)*	December

Patricia Reilly Giff is the author of many fine books for children, including the Kids of the Polk Street School books, The Lincoln Lions Band books, The Polka Dot Private Eye books, and the New Kids at the Polk Street School books. She lives in Weston, Connecticut.

DyAnne DiSalvo-Ryan has illustrated numerous books for children, including some she has written herself. She lives in Haddonfield, New Jersy.